MARSH-PAW PRESS

Other Books by Eric C. Harrison

Art

Blackened White
Art collection # 1

Denizens of Distraction
Art Collection # 2

Finding the Secret Sea
an experiment in spontaneity of image/word association
sketches by Eric C. Harrison with words by Mike Maguire

Writing

At The Bottom of The Big Top
A horror story told with poems.

MARSH-PAW PRESS

Available from Marsh Paw Press

www.marshpawpress.com

picture of a paranoid
by
Eric C. Harrison
Selected Poems, Prose & Short Stories, 2002-2012

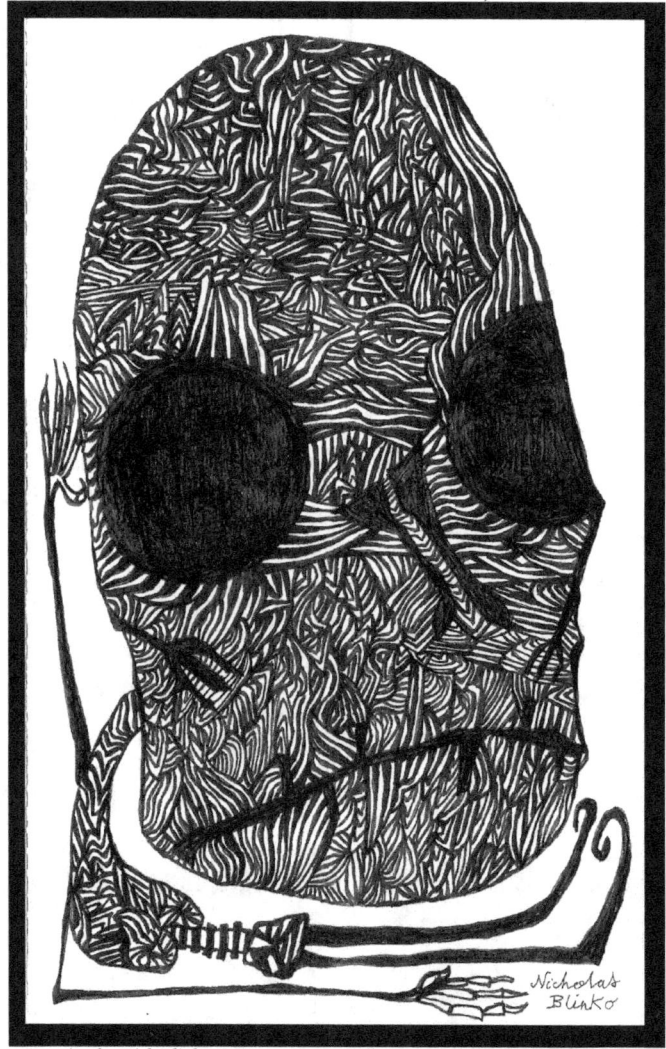

Drawing by Nick Blinko © Henry Boxer Gallery – reproduced with permission.

Marsh Paw-Press
2012

Picture of a Paranoid
Selected Poems, Prose & Short Stories, 2002-2012
Copyright © 2012, Eric C. Harrison

The majority of the pieces in this volume have been previously released in various forms of small-press. Some have been edited where it was possible to do so without altering the piece's intended point or original idea. A detailed list of acknowledgements outlining what has been previously published by whom, when and in what media can be found at the end of this book.

Many of these pieces were originally accompanied by dedications or tributes. The author feels that printing a dedication on the same page as a poem could interfere with an individual reader's interpretation of it. To prevent this, dedications were removed from the individual pages and now exist as a list which can also be found at the back of this book.

* Some of the prose pieces in this book are semi-fictitious. They contain real-life events & people that have been mixed with an equal number of complete falsities. This is generally intended as misdirection or humor. No insult, infringement or trespass of any kind is intended.

Cover art

"Skeleton Series #6"
Drawn by Nick Blinko

Circa 2000, ink on paper.
Copyright © Henry Boxer Gallery.
Original drawing owned by Eric C. Harrison.
Reproduced with permission.

* Marsh Paw Press logos by Eric C. Harrison © 2005/2012
*B9K9 band picture on last page by Eric C. Harrison © 2012

Published by
Marsh Paw Press
Massachusetts

ISBN 978-0-9888040-1-2

* First Print / First Edition Paperback - December, 2012.

Paranoid

paranoid

par-uh-noid

adjective

1. of, like, or suffering from paranoia.
1b.of, characterized by, or resembling paranoia
1c. Relating to, characteristic of, or affected with paranoia.

Noun

2. a person suffering from paranoia.

2b. a person who shows the behaviour patterns associated with paranoia

2c. n. One affected with paranoia.

Also, paranoiac (par-uh-noi-ak, -ik)
paranoeac (par-uh-nee-ak, -ik)

* informal exhibiting undue suspicion, fear of persecution

Origin: 1900–05; paranoi(a) + -oid, with base and suffix merged, perhaps by haplology from the expected *paranoioid

Origin - 1904, irregularly formed from paranoia + -oid. As a noun, "a paranoid person," attested from 1922.

Table of Contents

(Table of contents, continued.)

&#@%!

others

we are

freaks

see us

as if people

no

different than yourself

- 2003

Lost In Down-tuning

there are bridges in songs

built over headstones
that wear familiar

names and dates that call
memory back to life

like resurrection

forgotten marble teeth protrude
to feed on rootless flowers

thirst left barely slaked

by tears

places of rest
become silent
        lawns asleep

        to digest loved ones

           in trimmed green ground
           shovels dig deep

           mouths that yawn

                at death

                  - 2005

Ebenezer Oakman's House

Rise of the tide helps Atlantic water
reach past Point of Pines,
through Rumney Marsh
where it becomes brackish;
a river that flows with life in motion.

Mallards greet wood ducks among high reeds.
Cormorant fishes, breaks the surface.

Heron still by shore snags creek chub.
Gull drops clam on rock and feasts.

Railroad trestle rests quiet and dead.
Sulfur lingers in invisible mist.

Air pockets rise in a chorus of pops
through bottomless mud of low-tide bed.

Strong and stern
in its chipped, gray paint
Ebenezer Oakman's house
overlooks the waving dance
of cat-o'-nine and Bittersweet.

When mother nature hits these shores
she hits them hard,
leaves weather scars

but this cordwainer's home,
built in 1806
stands stubborn and proud,
refusing to budge.

- 2002

Paradox

Nemesis conundrum;

Concrete blocks (,)

hold (s) these

feet fast.

I wasn't born to follow.

I'll never be a leader.

- 2004

Domestic Oasis

tiger-tabby naps
seems as boneless as a doily
draped across a worn out pillow
snug and settled on tattered brown
couch arm graced by streams of cool

relief brought on by air-conditioner's
ingredient that's achieved domestic oasis

rats rest, lulled
in chilled chips of cedar
mice breathe easy under
soothe of ersatz breezes

dog circles
settles
on the floor
pants abate
as she gives in
to thoughts of water
that will still be cold
when she drinks

tail thumps a heavy
beat on hardwood
that slows, then stops
as her body surrenders

to sleep
    where in dreams
        she sees
        rabbits and chases

            - 2005

Diseased

immune to the poison
consumed for suppression
dulled by the stimulants
meant to obliterate
the perpetual pinch
of the thorn that digs in
and maintains its presence
through the weight of each step

father's day cards spit upon
dejected and torn
enmity's malediction evokes
wormwood on my tongue

subconscious guardian stands
behind murder-holes in my heart
baneful arrows collimate
the same name on each plume

fertilized by betrayal
memory weed germinates
roots raise bones from the ancient
graves believed to be forgotten

fire surges through shaken veins
diseased with bloodline curse

paroxysm of shameful truth
will not give up the ghost

"in that cold, crumbling house
you tried to steal away
something that belonged to you
but was never yours to take"

though one grants forgiveness
vindication remains with me

mature gestation of hate
awakens dormant madness

behind clenched eyes
ugly memories
spell out words
that won't wipe away
like WASH ME from a dusty car

      "If I don't send you to your grave
      I'll be there when you find it

      this book only closes
      with the lid of your coffin"

- 2002

Near the Door

It was very early Sunday morning.

The sun had only been up for a few minutes when a man and his dog reached Rising River.

The tide was high and the water was running strong. Bubbles swirled just below the surface; a deep blue strip of paisley with white detail.

Sunrise had given the marshlands a backdrop of fiery orange patches that were streaked with deep crimson. This dark red lingered beneath a layer of deepening, cadmium blue. It was a combination that made the early morning sky beautiful; in places like the tobacco sunburst of Gibson's Les Paul.

Overhead, a few thin clouds drifted above the general stillness that blanketed the surrounding neighborhood, which was not yet wholly awake. There were no other people out walking and very few cars were on the road.

As the amorphous puffs of white crossed the sky, dissipating as they went, the overall silence was suddenly disrupted by the squawking of many seagulls. They just suddenly appeared, circling overhead; a noisy flock of what seemed like nearly a hundred birds.

The gulls made their way to the Riverside Bar and Grill, where they swooped down to feed from the restaurant's dumpster. Saturday night was regularly a busy night at the Riverside, so the Sunday morning garbage was always worthwhile booty for these feathered pirates.

Some of the birds had to compete with the river rats that had already staked a claim on the same heap. Some of the larger gulls simply fed on the rats.

A large black-backed gull caught one of the gorged rodents by its hind leg and flew up above the parking lot. When it had lifted the rat about sixty feet above the ground it dropped the screeching animal from its blood covered beak. The rat landed on asphalt with a meaty thud. It twitched thirty seven times as life left it.

When the rodent's shattered body finally stopped moving, the gull that had dropped it flew down with the intention of eating it.

The other gulls, having heard the animal's death cries, also swooped down to feast.

Before the rat's killer could claim it, these other gulls were upon the carcass and tore the dead animal to pieces in seconds. There were so many birds fighting over one prize that none of them ended up with more than a taste.

Eventually, cars pulled into the lot as the restaurant's cleaning crew arrived. Both bird and rat alike retreated.

The man and his dog walked toward home, where they would enjoy a wonderful breakfast of their own.

Under the influence of the sun, the moon became more transparent with each minute; the fading face of a ghost in slow departure.

- 2005

Paranoid Haiku Sequence

paranoia time
when walls close with dark intent
thieves of final breath

liar behind shades
writes sad, tragic masterpiece
in which my life ends

pigs in mud grumble
devour all the happiness
that their snouts can find

when harsh sirens wail
I try, but can't stop thinking
they're coming for me

cold words of others
direct blunt innuendo
arrows at my heart

random cop cars pass
even on the bus I feel
their stare touching me

disappointed looks
sighs, frowns, displeased expressions
all scowls; meant for me

chemicals in food
make us return for our fix
while they kill us slow

lady on the train
looks me over, up and down
throws me a fake smile

business man makes room
keeps a distance between us
afraid I'll rob him

yuppie in silk threads
steps wide to one side; dodges
thinks I'm contagious

big brother watches
it waits to victimize me
for reasons unknown

met a girl on-line
but she's probably a guy
just fucking with me

look at a sick friend
who I know wants to die soon
to hurt my feelings

my dog is brighter
than he lets on; playing dumb
does require some smarts

you did not like these
poems, they might make you think
I'm idiotic

- 2004

True Last Call

too many people die alone
submerged in solitude
as they stare
down
at the end
of a long-neck or a fifth

    like a toast
    made to an empty room
    full of those remembered
    farewell feels so futile

        just a wave good-bye

        to a friend who's left

        in a cab that's turned the corner

- 2003

voices speak, live and go

open mind in whirlpools of media everywhere
blip dob dash dot com slash colon comma
choreographed split rainbow vibrations
theaters of electric bits and tree guts
ink well rage to program seduction
canvas board acrylic metaphors
flat pastel paper productions
cryptic expression, line lie
colliding worlds in wash
hues caught in plastic
linguistic puzzle box
oil color espionage
physical fantasies
dream equations
opaque visions
word glowing
mind exiting
host matter
takes root
sounds
voices
speak
live
and
go
!

- 2002

Interlude of Pointless observations #1

Cable Television;

"_Previously_

on the   _history_   channel ... "

- vaguely redundant.

- 2012

Rusted Heads Rise

nails pull up slowly
through unpainted wood
slats stepped on daily
by light and heavy

shoes, boots and sneakers
on the feet of life
        seekers
        in entry
        or exit
        exposed
            to sun
                shine
                on the porch
                at moon's departure

                  as rusted heads rise

                        in slow motion

                          asunder

                        - 2005

Paper Shadow Shredder

To feel better,
reduce

problems; turn them
into calculations.

Contain them
on pages
in books
as paper
    to be
        burned

in fearful dark hours
where cadence becomes
knock and pound
of unseen drum-
beats that rise
up from under

ground as it shifts
to release
miasmal music
that clouds and blurs

direction needed
to avoid feeling

the appetite that fuels the Tick-Tock Crocodile.

- 2005

walk WITH dog

under boot and paw
the rhythmic
crunch of gravel
creates tempo

to a wordless song
carried between
two companions in harmony

togetherness is a melody
perfectly tuned by trust

in footsteps
        an age-old measure of   friendship
        when shared over time   two become one

                              instrument
                              that eliminates
                              the need to speak

- 2003

sometimes I wonder if I want them to

shield me with dark glasses
to keep my eyes   from inquiry
that would bring the dam to crumble

I do not belong in this society
this world
this mess
this ruined place
            where all I do is fuck up

sometimes I wonder if I want them to

quiet this mind
this suspicious
paranoid   idiot voice

sometimes I wonder if I want them to

burn this chaotic carousel
with its mock-talking riders

devil fingers that prod
and point out things
I don't want to see

horses ablaze
spin in circles

the air they pass through
                  feeds the fire

- 2002

Musical Midwives

self-prescribed headphones
drown sickness that spews

poison from mouths that surround
to spread curses, stress contagious

word plague that flies like bats disturbed
by flicker of torchlight's dance on cave walls

shut out the world in transformation
scream to whisper; calm from clamorous

musical midwives cut the cord
as notes and melody harmonize

with dream, drift to secluded space
between and in, where drums embrace

song's concrete elimination
of petty fucking shit

- 2003

Death Under The 107 Bridge

One place of my youth;
107 highway bridge
Built on Rumney Marsh.

Atlantic Lobster
nearby, now an empty shell
where all kinds dropped lines.

In brackish water
Striper, Pollock, Flounder, Chubs
Sea-Robins, Tautog,

crazed Bluefish that charged
up river, after herring,
to feed in frenzy.

Fins would break surface
as the Blues hit from under
unwary bait-fish.

Mostly, people talked.
Strangers not so strange when we
all were there to fish.

Everyone burned slow
under summer sun that drummed
down on spring-soft skins.

Every body stunk
of fish, sweat, beer, smoke or fumes
from cars that whizzed by.

When the tide shifted
we'd run across the highway
to catch the outflow.

We were ALL anglers;
Sportsmen, drunks, yuppies, kids, adults
old men with secrets.

All walks of life came
to the bridge now devoid of
fishermen and fish.

Dead rivulet fades
filled with junk and pollution
from the Resco plant.

Riverbed graveyard
shows headstone of fishery;
the murder victim.

– 2003

To Hear Pan

coax life from
a corpse, still

buried in night's lonesome
quiet, primal composition

sit with Pan
draw dark
harmony
out of poison
pipes, pour sour

songs with each breath
like notes in a dream song
played on ancient dead wood

winds that carry magic
bouquets of extinct
flowers used as brushes

paint delicate memories
in and over time
covet the ability

to create temptation's portrait
stir enough embers
to see the need

for freedom
                    transcend reserve

                                        - 2004

November 3rd, 2004

Behind Boston
Street Café,

the unemployed
sit in

un-sober sanctuary
parked cars give them

beside Saugus River
engines run
ready for exodus
when cruisers flash blue

lights, sirens
interrupt those empty

days filled
with too much
free

time
    to relish

        the beauty
        of a paper bag

            mask that covers
            bottled breakfast

                - 2004 (wow, imagine that.)

Among Monsters

Sometimes, when I look outside
at comfortable lamp lit streets
shaded enough to drown colors,
silent cars and sleeping houses,

alienation's face greets me
on a pane of glass made opaque
by the grayscale world beyond.

There are so many things to avoid
along the frightful busy
sidewalks crowded with thieves

charlatans that sell fools gold,
paste pearls. On diseased whores
with shitty drugs for crazy, dangerous

lunatic wolves that wear slick
musky sheepskin and smile-traps
made to bite unwary stargazers.

I drift
through morning
when people have just started

off into their days. They are
still tired and too busy
to fuck anyone over.

I find myself hidden behind
music under hood drawn up
over my head to darken all

with a scowl that casts
daggers to make deadly
radius out of hope
none will approach.

At night,
among these monsters
half asleep and vulnerable,

I stare at words
in a book
on my lap;

pre-occupied,
paranoid
to the point

that pages appear
to hold nothing but letters

adrift alphabet soup.

- 2003

Interlude Of Pointless Observations #2: American Batman

On page 206 of the Vintage Contemporaries 1st Edition, perfect-bound, US paperback version of American Psycho (by Bret Easton Ellis © March, 1991) the main character, a maniacally obsessive and homicidal (but superbly dressed and well mannered) yuppie by the name of Patrick Bateman, is referred to (playfully, I believe) as "Batman" by one of his many upper-crust acquaintances, whom he encounters in one of the many high-end nightclubs or restaurants that he is known to frequent.

On April 14th 2000 an adaptation of American Psycho was released as a major motion picture production (directed by Mary Harron and released by Lions Gate Films) and was made available on DVD by September of the same year. The now-available "Killer Edition" DVD includes a number of enjoyable deleted scenes as well as some witty commentary by the cast and crew.

In American Psycho, the movie, the actor Christian Bale takes on the role of the murderous Patrick Bateman. Though Bale is brilliant and the movie is enjoyable, it pales in comparison to Ellis's fantastic book.

Ironically, in 2005 Bale (whose drive for physical fitness appears to have superseded even that of the health obsessed Bateman) plays the role of Bruce Wayne, aka Batman, in the fourth (and best, in my opinion) Batman movie which is called "Batman Begins" (story by David S. Goyer, directed by Christopher Nolan, released by Warner Brothers).

So, Bateman was called Batman in the book *and,* as irony would have it, the character of Batman is eventually portrayed by the same actor who played Bateman in the movie.

Bateman was called Batman,
Bales became Bateman
then Bales became Batman
(and in being Batman, also Bruce).

So,
Bateman, through Bales,
became Batman and Bruce.

Bateman, Batman, Bales, Bateman/Batman/Bruce ...

I have it on good authority that *they* did all this just to fuck with me and that someone who may end up reading this self-indulgent, little piece-of-crap blurb could have been in on the plot.

- 2006

in the orchard

shrunken life fleshed out

that day; we both were giant

hearts about Cortlands

- 2010

Chuckleberry Finn

First they chase each other.

The Butterfly Hunter barrels after The Mouse Hunter.

The Mouse Hunter only wants a few seconds to piss in peace. A vicious snarl and lunging snap give him those few seconds.

His golden haired adversary backs away slowly, dramatically playing out "fear" in each carefully placed backward step, to keep the game friendly.

Relieved, the Rat Terrier leaps up, to play-nip at a blonde floppy ear. The Golden retriever ducks his head and contact fails.

In their tussle a small bunch of leaves is kicked up into the strong April wind. Dry as paper, one of these takes flight.

The dogs stop, momentarily statuesque. Then their eyes move in perfect unison. Their vision follows the pattern of the air-born leaf. Neither dog blinks.

Up and up the leaf goes and suddenly it's carried quickly across the yard and the competing canines make chase.

Both dogs jump up and bite at the leaf, trying to catch it in their mouths. The leaf blows over the back steps and the dog's nails clack as they climb the wooden flight in pursuit.

The leaf manages to catch on a hanging metal and glass candle-lantern, which dangles from one of the eaves over the porch.

The dogs freeze again, their mouths open, their expressions dead-set and serious.

The wind picks up. The lantern sways and the leaf is blown free. It circles, loops and dips right into Chuck's path and he snatches it.

Then the twenty pound terrier prances back and forth in front of his competition. His little victory strut announces that the prize has been won and who has won it.

The retriever's eighty some-odd pounds wiggle. His golden behind actually swings back and forth, caught in the momentum of his furiously wagging tail. His big, webbed paws step up and down, up and down - he doesn't know what to do; run, jump, lunge or watch?

Dargo is just so happy about having fun and excited about the game itself, that at one point - when Chuck, teasing, pretends to drop the leaf - Dargo flinches and nearly throws himself off balance.

Suddenly, Chuck seems to realize that having the dead leaf is nothing to gloat about. It is not all that he thought it would be. It's just a leaf, after all and tastes almost like nothing. It has no chew to it. It is brittle, frail.

But, Chuck wants to keep Dargo envious, so he chews the leaf anyway. He acts as if the dried husk is as savory as a slice of American Cheese. He wags his little thumb-sized nub of a tail as he chews. His eyes are half-closed in mock- ecstasy.

Watching, I start to think of Chuck as Chuckleberry Finn, even though it's really Tom Sawyer that I'm thinking of. Chuckleberry is just a more natural play on the little dog's name.

Specifically, I'm reminded of how Tom had made his whitewashing chores seem enjoyable in order to trick other boys into doing the work for him. I'm thinking about how he'd even gotten some of the kids to give him gifts as a trade-off or payment for a go at the job.

Chuck will go on being called Chuckleberry from time to time, but being a Rat Terrier certainly makes him more like the evil Sawyer lad. It's Dargo that's more like Huck, who saw everything in life as something good.

And after all, I am certain, beyond a reasonable doubt, that Chuck would happily exchange a chance to chew on the dried out leaf for *"a dead rat and a string to swing it on"* or *"a kitten with only one eye."*

- 2008

Hurling Coin

another coin toss moment
during "edge of seat" feeling
each minute as an eternal

flip in the drop

aches and pains call heads
welfare again stuck with tails.

chance died as a false concept

just polite
words, really false

promises to navigate
puddles of ink
that bleed from wet sentences

documents dried out
to kindle

aspiration between
secret covers
pushed to corners

pounded into submission
molested
bled

better judgment,
            unconscious
                    near coffer

blind
horse follows
led

old trick, new carrot

decisions sway
heavy gravy

lies stand out
as abrasive
messages
in plumes of steam
off of shit
in yellow snow

one, idiopathic, buys them all
cuts coupons marked Rx

consideration trims the platter

enjoyable self - testing

mad-scientist-lab-rat-freak

- 2002

Chapbook Chimney

another page of Grimoire

turns, marked forever
in permanent ink; the gone

one's John Hancock; written
on the wall
labeled "W A S"

February thin, Sunday tired
black crows gather
at chimney's rim

the red pillar juts
from the rooftop, skyward
it puffs gray
wisps of smoke

a barrel-fire that warms
filthy hands of the faceless
bundled up nomadic
inhabitants of the cold
dirty, dark
truth

of her remains

        pages that will flip forever
        to warm a flock of blackbird poets
        huddled around her chapbook chimney

- 2005

The feel of the Bridge

a new day's field
bears golden gift;
                    star-fire on the up-rise

copper glimmer shimmers on liquid
adder that winds
through cord-grass
which leads to

rusted,   devoured bridge of   ancient
box-cars,   trains now dead,   silent
still   remain strong,   monumental

in passage over
bones of wood
steel plate skin

the dog is leery
as we cross
her toes feel differences
lost to shoe-foot;

                    vibrations change with the tide
                    shake barnacle covered support
                    beams beneath the yellow
                    sun that gives this trestle warmth

                    and   the damp night air's
                    cold   that remains
                    settled   in metal plate
                    under   sensitive
                    paws
                                        - 2003

No Rooster

mourning comes after

sun sets

to hide

        it

      drops

      down

(behind)
      trees that shade

          a forest
          of houses

          flesh of their dead

          ancestors

- 2002

Ambivalent

she makes it hard

to enjoy sex

fuck her

2003

THUMBPRINT

reflected off pools of weird, cool water
born from creeks on mountains once molehills
histrionic mud pies grew up and left home
now frightened insects rise above without regard

crumbled foundation shows traces of what was
head house burned to ground, aged parchment

reserve bodies, soaked with gasoline dry in the sun
ignition spells out my name, past and present

man's devil pisses napalm onto newborn goals
burnt aspirations scream fruitlessly for help

old gods ignore new, blind idiot's gibbering prayer
bitter pagan entities jealous of the jesus fan club

longboats sink, vessels crafted to touch bottom
made to die, sentient meat-on-four-legs mooing

compelled to shit out ugly lies, hopeless innuendoes
maps lead to edges of worlds plotted with cruel intent

captain's quarters abandoned, no one at the helm
sharp rocks up ahead pose as comfortable chairs

guilty fools keel haul selves as others dance the plank
hopes for injury's given way to medicated whirlpool

newspaper sails twist out tales of turbulent
unreadable fine print written in foreign tongues

illiterate sailors depressed over lack of pictures
fumble loose pages; torn, dog eared, yellowed, stained

thumb prints adorn August pinup whore in sweat shop
worry across minds that wonder if she's truly a nice girl

what brought this damsel to the pages of jack-off city
from untainted peaks
of virgin times
          when hopes were real

                        - 2002

Ends In Silent Battle

In a shaded glen a beautiful young woman with very long auburn hair knelt before a dark pool of water. Her palms pressed into soft peat as she leaned forward to take a drink.

The bog was still and calm. As the girl sipped from the pool, she appeared to kiss an identical twin sister, who existed in an upside-down place where life went on beneath a layer of glass.

Perhaps they each wondered, when their full lips met, if the other recognized the unseen divide between the worlds they each occupied.

The peat beneath them was saturated and groundwater simultaneously ran up between their fingers.

The surrounding forest's floor was littered with dead branches and dry leaves. The place was primarily populated by ferns, enormous oaks trees and cranberry bushes.

Cardinals and jays flitted about on branches overhead while sparrows, robins and grackles ran or hopped back and forth on the ground.

These birds were a spectrum of feathered motion and seemed to be wrapped up in a debate which involved some sort of bird politics;

"My seed here, your seed there ... Peck not on my land and I shall peck not on yours ... thou shalt respect the earliest bird ..." and so forth.

Nearby, on the tips of dead trees which protruded from the mud like gray-brown fingers of giant zombies frozen in mid-escape from their graves, a hungry murder of black crows waited for something, anything, to die.

Lichen occupied the bases of trees while decade old ivy climbed vertical trunks, gripping bark in undetected motion; as if in answer to the call of the sun, it ventured upward.

A bouquet born of apples which decorated a nearby tree mingled with the perfume of an enormous lilac bush that was rooted in the nutritious soil beneath the rotted trunk of an enormous toppled Oak.

This fallen tree was laid out, limbs spread; a gigantic, deteriorating corpse. It was decorated with toadstools and clusters of bright orange and yellow mushrooms.

A third generation Trumpet Vine worked slowly to dominate the north end of this decaying mammoth. But its competition, a young and ambitious Morning Glory, rich with purple, star-like flowers, was giving it a run for its money.

- 2005

Dulled by Wooden Owls

featureless faces on half-dead dream boxes
long for mouths with which they would taste
salt of tears in exodus from eyes unknown to drip

along non-existent bridges which deny sweet
scents to enter and stimulate those once numb
minds born like babies un-slapped at delivery

forget to breathe and die right there on flat steel
tables where hearts stop, flesh cools with settling
bones - undeveloped and soft but naturally able

to take a fall without fracture or fatality - just
imagine; the bland life of Tarot's fool at cliff's
edge, to step off, head high among thin clouds

to occupy cobalt skies until gravity takes
hold without threat of suffering the outcome
as pain's beacon of life flickers out; dulled wall

paper; flat bland patterns meant to push lost pupils
with the lightest touch; silent, moot distractions
roof-bound wooden owls that crows no longer fear

- 2005

Warm Gift of Snow

bitterness neutralized in coffee
touched with cream and sugar's base
blankets that fall and push down
hypothermic winter worms

into layers that keep the cold at bay
hurried feet that carry those warm
bodies grown fat from holiday feasts
through chilled air in heavy coats

collars up, hats pulled down
hidden faces; anonymous, shadowed
eyes peer over scarfs adjusted
gloves and mittens cover fingers

over sidewalks footprints left
by unseen boots decorated in salt's
strange white patterns; crystalized Rorschach
erosion that eats away shoes, roads and cars

on tracks that network frozen ground
locomotive men and women
breathe steam into the air
destination; hearth and home

- 2004

Picture of you

before sleep
arrives   routine

rituals that build
blockades against insomnia

beneath thick clouds
varied smoke

mismatched sheets cover windows
kill the sun, drench the room

with darkness or the glow of television
in a state of white noise illumination

a choir-girl often sings to me
as I struggle for slumber
I hear her whisper

in magic equations;
reminders of love's value
to commiserate solitude

with tender songs that bury the ugly
sounds of the world beyond thin walls

she unlocks ducts with ivory keys
opens reservoirs that quiver with need

to release tension that dams a flood of tears
that would otherwise drown the sleeper in dreams

in
the comfort of dim

light, I lay back
to drift off as sleepy
            eyes   droop but remain

            fixed on a screen
            where pixels produce
            an image

                  - your smile
                        aglow

            it reaches with tender
            beauty that guides me

            past nightmares and onward
            to pleasant vistas

                  where you warm
                  my blankets
                  and place
                        an invisible hand
                        over my tired heart

                              -2003

Under The Arbor

under the arbor two peepers
drink Creeley in
sunlight that seeps
between thick green
leaves to feed
sour grape vines that weave
together; wrap down
to entangle wooden
bench that seats just one

bare toes touch moist
clover pillow grown thick
in deep shadows that shelter
a large paw-dug dirt-bed
where days are dreamed away

October finds our home overseen
by busy squirrels that live
in a marmalade maple neurotic neighbors
that forage and scramble
to win a frantic race against
rakes that threaten
to steal precious acorns

marigolds bloom near imperfect
grayed steps built two years back
by the same tired hands
that raise coffee to lips
and then light a smoke
while true blue companion
reads motion among branches

- 2003

In The Vicinity Of Death

twelve and seven inch records collected
reach across time
over the years

their covers have gathered
layers of dust

in an attic
behind stacks of
water warped boxes
that hold old, pale, flat
psychedelic pictures

near rusted rat trap
jaws that cling
to shattered skeletons
of the long dead
tempted vermin
speak of things
gathered and held

a legacy of sorts
that will fade away
like those bones of the fallen

treasures that at best will be
barely glanced at
while swept into dustpans

by hurried brooms
held within callous
hands of total strangers

- 2005

So I Believe

so what if I believe in magic

things that never were
seen by skeptical
closed eyes open

laugh at me
as I chase pixies
alive in my garden
beneath tiger lilies
where tiny footprints tell the truth

if only I could shrink down small
take her hand and run away
to peaceful glens
where ferns give shelter

from the world of hypocrite's
belief in christ
who walked on water
but not in faeries
or their   tales

we could hide forever knowing
the word is not in the bible
but in bark grown thick
on a tree called life

a secret *concealed* from non-believers

- 2002

c a T H e r I N e

dull, dreary fade

stakes claim on blue

fabric
         loosened with age

       worn
       yet already wearing

       thin
       torn up
           weave hangs
            nearly floats

           over hips, reveals
           curve, shows bone

downcast eyes tell
a story grown common

as laughter grew louder
insecurity starved her

                  - 2003

Retrieving

days once treasured   lost to dog-death
joy smothered under   dark shadow's blanket

empty hours that enhance   wounds to show
time does not heal   it just strengthens

                tolerance

with heavy thread that cloaks   to coddle
resident gloom which eats   like a shark

in blood riven frenzy,   it digests each
color swallowed to distract from inner picture

                  distorted
             disoriented
         tear-blind

sailor 's eye gazes
toward moon and stars
navigates un-sturdy
vessel, finds failure

bow-maiden
blistered with barnacles
cries
mark twain for the human anchor

whose one last breath
a gasp that will bring
the end
as lungs fill up with water

days of discordance
in lonesome wander

crying-jag memoirs
adorn every corner

labyrinthine tunnels
boast hypnotic graffiti

memories
like mice in the marsh grass
stir

sense of recall; a half-starved hawk

golden retriever pup joins daily journey
calls on bloodhound of hunter heritage

in the face of stagnant quagmires
where melancholy pools

this web-toed water-dog
wades
through the dark
deep with a wag

sniffs out
retrieves

smiles
thought lost

- 2007

Brown's House

Three lawns down
at the slight curve
of a hill's north slope
dogwood grows
where Brown's house sits
humble and hidden.

On the lawn
a small sign tells of a shoe
merchant who lived in
1832.
These painted
numbers and letters draw view
to a birdhouse atop
the same wooden post.

The east side ground dips
deep to form
a rich green dish
of mother earth
where shrubs give shade
to Black-Eyed Susan
sentries that stand steady guard.

Each winter its ancient foundation supports
a Colonial home in defiance of time

> and it reminds us
> that, It - like those
> well-maintained walls
> covered in Frost
> poems, will last
> hundreds of years.   - 2003

Interlude Of Pointless Observations #3 - BOOZE

In Massachusetts it's not uncommon to go into a liquor store to buy an alcoholic beverage and be turned away because you show them that you're of age with a State ID.

Many liquor stores even post signs near the entrance or at the register that indicate that the establishment will not accept a Mass State ID as a form of identification.

It is also not uncommon to walk into a bar and not be served because you only have a Massachusetts State ID as opposed to a Massachusetts State Driver's License.

The Registry used to issue what was called a State Liquor License and those are both accepted by both liquor stores and bars. However, the last time I tried to get one I was told they were no longer issued. I've heard that they have reinstated the liquor license or will be doing so in the future.

Though I rarely drink, I find it the idea of denying a person the booze they want because he or she does not have a driver's license to be really fucking stupid.

Essentially it means that the grounds of denial are based on a person not being a driver.

This boils down to is the dangerous and frightening concept that in order to drink - you HAVE to drive.

The last time I checked these two activities were not known as being the greatest combination.

- 2005

Pink Mittens On The Train

she reads Harry Potter
turns pages with pink mittens

her scarf, a candy-colored cloth
bright and sweet like Za-Rex

a pom-pom on her winter cap
hot chocolate sipped with a smile

worn out, canvas tote bag holds
high heeled shoes, vanilla yogurt

blue eyes shift and express
emotions drawn from words

between the covers, she's become
completely lost in fairy tales

sometimes a gasp, a giggle or
true worry haunts her eyes

suspense that brings her
to the edge of her seat

where she hangs
with perfect posture

2004

Snowflakes Melt

to have nobody

understand what you are

going through ... a feeling

everyone knows

2004

A Today of 23 Years

in errand run
on main street, small town
see what's there
as if it were veiled
behind apparitions
of what once was
                and what is there no more

dollar store and nail boutique
mask the old Granada Theater
where hand carved balustrades lined velvety red
carpet that rose and spiraled with flight
of wide stairs that wound toward a chandelier
fancy balconies and old-school opera seats

these were two-bit luxuries
but why waste a quarter?
kids are great sneaks

flicks were a dollar and that buck kept us
happy all day in repeat view of movies
until film's dialog could be recited
line for line before words escaped
the sound system's speakers, old and outdated

great to the ears of a child who hears
through imagination which filters
flaws found in stone-age, caveman-cinema

an old, familiar stairwell
caught in peripheral
swims up from under
like a catfish to feed on
the cliché burden of
Atlas as it shrivels
to childhood Sunday
bowling with bio-dad
asshole's regular, inexpensive
way of killing the two
visitation hours supposedly cherished

remember centipede, played that very first time
virgin strike, second spare, seven-ten, gutter ball

automat style machines once served
hot coffee, cocoa, chicken broth, tea
cold cola, seltzer, old fountain style
orange soda that always went flat
these all washed down plastic
bagged snacks, somehow stale

no bond, just pawned
off to places
no mentor to teach me
to fly-fish for deer or hunt for trout
or how to track and snare the invisible
elusive concept of quality time

- 2003

Wooden Time Machine

an old junk drawer is a time machine
the past lay buried
beneath yellowed papers

restaurant menus, receipts and dead batteries
bills so outdated
their debt now seems minor

a full book of matches from the old Jerry Jingle's
no longer grilling,
long since torn down

Saint Paulie girl coaster, another marked Schlitz
tell tales of old taste when the poison was beer

brass subway tokens from a trip to New York
before stigma of terror took two towers down
bring quick recollection
of child's perception
bored by a long trip
trapped in a car

boat by the falls on a souvenir magnet
Maid of The Mist says Niagara vacation

church key opens memory to first hard drink
taken with parents, in toast to ... something

key-rings with keys that no longer have locks
some shine like new
others lack luster

separated from secrets
behind seldom scathed tumblers
of hackneyed old padlocks
on crates in the attic

old polaroid photo
of friends in a huddle
shot out of focus

in a phase of rebellion
now moot self-expression

out-of-style haircuts, outdated clothing
Kinks t-shirt won at a carnival dart toss

a pen and blank paper
next year's unmarked

calendar time capsule
spaces hold
unborn nostalgia

- 2003

Shooting Star

When a cow can
    "Jump over"

    (said cow)
    the MOO n   births lunar

    boredom's vampire

        to strike
   and sap *a little*
       star, its twinkle turns to

slag dold r u m s . . .

days of astrology   (invariable, inevitable)
mysteries (monstrosities)

   vomited into
         science to dissect
  those who tempt *heavenly bodies*
         with education's

     sorcery

they tear down
curtains that hide

gadgets to produce charlatan magic

when I   wished upon

a (fatal)   SHOO Ting
         STAR

She came
For the showdown

Donned mother goose
Guns Greased

lightning sleight
    of hand Slapped
        Leather holsters   slung

from garter belts hung
over spurred spike heels

death draw   dropped

        denim bags of *flesh*
            in dust-
        clouds to die

    on the street

    of

  a   ghost   town

where   fantasy   will have

this   delusional   desperado

in retirement   bleeding from

    dreams

        - 2004

Interlude of Pointless Observations # 4

Whoever it was that first said

    "There are no stupid questions"

        probably asked a lot of them.

- 2012

Dead Dragonflies

"blonder" makes my eyes as dry
as dead collected dragonflies

fixed and locked in
perpetual   stare

beauty   sometimes, under scowl

                    threaten to kick the ass of my heart
                    and I'd throw in the towel

sometimes morning found you
blipping pokes as you got dressed
with tales of your cats
their tails in your lap
        (lucky cats ...)
left me wishing
I could speak
        "purr"
or that I was a spider
or a scorpion that knows
Doolittle has nothing over
that spot on your soul   for   animals
                            over people
                            it creates vacancy
                            for you within the heart

        though there could not be much more
            of your beauty,   there's so much

                    more to you than that

                            - 2003

AOC Memory

There's one small spot in front of The Knitting Factory
under an eave. Out of the rain. Shielded from wind.

People, hurried along by the rain, pass without seeing
this spot. Two lovers huddle together and share an
umbrella. They almost seem to wear one coat. The man
has one arm over the girls shoulder. Their cheeks press
close. They are only aware of each other.

A man comes out of The Knitting Factory. The door
swings slowly shut behind him and the sound of voices
mixed with music fades to silence. The street's noise
seems to return to full volume.

The man steps into the sheltered area. He does this with
familiarity. No glancing around, no second thoughts.

He turns his collar up and pulls a Sherlock Holmes style
pipe out of his coat along with a drawstring pouch. He
takes tobacco out of this and tamps the brown weed into
the pipe.

The pipe dangles from his mouth. Its stem is clenched
between his teeth and he appears to grin painfully. The
bowl bobs and tips a bit as he fishes a box of hurricane
matches out of his pocket.

A few bits of tobacco escape the bowl and fall onto
reflections of red, yellow and green lights that decorate
the wet pavement.

A match is lit and raised to the pipe and the man begins
to puff. The tobacco is damp and does not ignite at first.

The flame consumes the matchstick and nearly burns the man's fingers. He drops the match and avoids being singed.

When the tobacco is beginning to light someone says,

"I've never seen such a young guy smoking a pipe like that."

The man holds a new, lit match over the bowl with very steady hands. The flame barely wavers.

He seems to nod in agreement with his entire upper body; his shoulders stiffly moving up and down. His hands cup around the pipe, one of them manipulates the lit match. He avoids bending his neck.

Finally looks toward the speaker. He has friendly eyes. His lips smile around the stem of the pipe. It is a warm smile. His expression is one that says he's heard this comment before and that it pleases him.

Smoke rises as the man stands up straight. His body relaxes as he frees a cloud from his lungs into the rainy night air. The smoke drifts down the street and passes over three ticketed, illegally parked cars before it disappears.

The man grips the pipe by pinching the base of the bowl between his thumb and forefinger. He takes it out of his mouth and says "Just down here to the right," he points the stem of the pipe toward some unseen spot off in the distance of the great grid that is New York and says "is Great Jones Avenue. It's a famous place."

He takes another puff on his pipe and corrects himself. "Well, it's infamous really. It is a notorious place, it's um ... associated with heroin. A street of ill repute." He rolls the r's on 'street' and 'repute' with theatric flare.

His eyes are now gleeful. His smile is wider but somehow he seems a little less friendly, more smug.

No one has said anything else to the man with the pipe but he goes on anyway. "It's where the term Jones comes from. Like, I've got a Jones running through my bones."

He puffs a little more. When he exhales he smiles as if remembering something wonderful from long ago.

"I carry this" he motions with the pipe, up and toward the person who had spoken to him. The gesture is done in much the same way that a person at a party might raise a glass to a friend they recognize on the other side of a room that would take forever to cross . "So that when the clubs and stores close and I'm Jonesing for tobacco, I'm good to go" he concludes

And off he goes.

The speaker says nothing.

- 2010

Trout Garden

beneath rosebuds
spade turns over
sun dried soil
in search of moisture

within garden
that brings beauty
peaceful colors

food for food

earthworms wriggle
in mulch and dirt
picked like fruit
to be consumed

when exchanged
for rainbow trout
through simple rule

"just add water"

- 2004

Ligament from page 15

* Cue Music:
Gypsies Tramps and Thieves,
Cher -1970-71

reproduced
on a handsome

167f roll driven carousel
punk band organ
with marching bass boom bash
terrifying tympani beater
scary snare drum
spinal tap & roll
cymbal car crash
& corpse twitch rhythm

Bermuda triangle tingles
timed with creepy
calm-killing castanets

43 reed calliope pipes
that preach back-wood gadget gospel
backed by a 27 note glockenspiel choir

beautiful clockwork, gargantuan gizmo
6 feet tall
9 feet wide
3 feet deep
350 pounds

towed by 30 trained poodles in frill

- 2006

In The Midst

confused, ring master caught
in shuffle spins. arms and mind akimbo
shot and killed with small clown from cannon

darkness and motion fill canvas, cavernous
lung of Big-Top - it breathes foul
putrescent air produced
by bodies that writhe as if newborn
maggots behind thin, membranous walls

animals escape in the midst of confusion
elephants trample crooked vendors and kiosks
jumbos crush stale popcorn and leaky balloons

mammoths remember Lil' Tyke and attack
trunks swing to break ribs, dulled tusks impale
feet pound and send ripples through fresh pools of blood

monkeys loot peanuts, tear apart cotton candy
sellers who peddle pink fiberglass tufts
lions and tigers follow clothed dancing grizzly
mammals maul vulnerable; screaming children

slow moving, elderly folks clutch at their chests
drop canes, spit false teeth as beast's jaws sink in

black market black bears dance through 3 ring buffet
self-serve a gluttonous feast of sweet revenge
once shackled and caged, now on top of the chain
enormous striped cat chokes to death on pace maker

king of the jungle shows disgusted expression
roars out his dislike of the taste of prosthetics   - 2006

FC

seven hundred days sounds like a lot

until weighed in pounds
measured in inches
stored in boxes
divided with seasons
or calculated with equation

then it seems like nothing

take that time

to

obsess over errors
choke on regret
dredge through burden
get slammed in the fucking face
run circles in your mind
fumble blind for reason

then it seems like seven hundred years

-2002

In Massachusetts

rock doves huddled
clothe snow covered window

ice blurred panes of glass above
sills not decorated by feathers
shaken loose in flight

instead they boast
the bloated, plump, frozen
stiff, still bodies of the city

birds lost
to nature's cold
that left them crystallized

beach-sand melted
reformed as pretty
baubles that will never shine

untalented actors played as pawns
inconsequential, names forgotten

fools to murder
lay with kings
felled like trees
by their shattered
valueless thrones of carnival glass
that reveal hidden edges
and cut when in shards

like a pickle dish known to Ethan Frome

- 2005

caduceus coyote

It runs half empty with a wrench in the engine;
a machine that slows and falters at every new corner,
each bend finds errors and breaks in its structure.

Croaker walks heavy, up and down a weak ladder,
injects opiate ice to dull coals that feed spine-
fire; felt from the tailbone to the base of the skull.

A rubber dam blocks a river of conductors
as the last electric ripples break the surface
in pulses; rings that spread outward and fade.

Capsules become Babylonian bricks, create walls
that rise into the sky; where digits grow and extend
to touch cool water that runs down ancient mountains.

Foundation set deep in the dirt builds itself. Downward,
like a spreading cancer, it races toward the earth's
core to be cauterized in magma; sealed and polished.

A troll inside, smells air that grows thin and learns to fear
suffocation; the new enemy marches slowly into reality,
steals oxygen through the rapid breaths of adversaries.

Outside a cripple sees freshly severed legs that dance,
as a motorized wheelchair outruns a pack of wild colts
to the glue factory, in hopes of compensation for bones.

Vertebrae slither from the body's restriction,
find a rock in the desert where they lay out to dry
under sun to be snatched by caduceus coyote.

Mundane secrets, of little concern, told in full
to us, as we lay perfectly still; "to be dead takes away
the pain" these lies translated with stucco and cracks.

Now ... numb,

left
to look

up
at the ceiling,

a man
wrapped
in bandages

laughs.

- 2003

Where Bees and Creatures Greet

short-lived brilliant colors of crepuscule
fade to complete darkness and grow
secure that silent voices touch
like lover's whispered tones that wake

sun flowers tomorrow as morning bodies
rise to stretch among lush gardens
where overgrown paths have lost the way
in the efflorescence that struggles through
veils that block signals from vast worlds beyond

soft soil nanny who nurses tender
roots, makes beds for bulbs and stalks

that dance in the breeze
under porch-lamp's white beams
mixed with full moon's silver bath
where shift of tincture paints brand new
magical faces that smile for a savior

whose parasol shades the frightened
eyes that dilate in the high felt

as reality falls into pitch and leaves
clamor behind covers echo

heard by us, alone
in faerie fire aglow

equipoised in the moment's spotlight
bee and creature greet

- 2005

cigar box polaroid

once a tobacco trove

now a cradle of keepsakes

boxed away memory flares

set glow to nostalgia

2003

Trod On Dead Being Gone

cold gray bodies
under ground buried
alive

one who failed
died, still
tried to scratch
to the sun through silk
smooth

lies
beneath the polished
lid of coffin

wood
we pave over

smoke stained skeletons
scattered; the bones of those long gone
tribes whose footprints are filled
with ashen cremains
                corpses will always be

            felt   in thick, heavy
                    breaths that rise
                    upward through
                    the rot of those endless

                    piles of ugly

                    wilted dead flowers

                            - 2005

Howard and Eleanor

Eleanor always gives me the same cold, reptilian stare when I drink my wine. She has a sort of signature facial expression; unblinking and condescending it wordlessly says - "Drinking AGAIN, Howard?!"

The walls of my skull can barely withstand even the mere thought of her grating voice - so her stare is, unfortunately for me, very affective.

When she actually vocalizes those words - each syllable is accompanied by the strong sensation that my teeth, which often clench involuntarily as she annunciates, are vibrating with a growing intensity that will eventually cause them to shatter.

Her wretched squeal sincerely makes my brain quiver and my head threaten to implode. As soon as the words leave her lips I feel a migraine coming on that is comparable to the sort of cranial discomfort that sets in gradually when gasoline or solvent fumes are inhaled in an enclosed space. Like when a person who has breathed unhealthy, chemical filled air (... who had probably forgotten to properly ventilate in the first place) feels the start of what will be one killer headache that silently promises to leave a trail of permanent brain damage in its wake.

But, regardless of Eleanor's disapproval, I know what I enjoy. So each night I ignore the selfish lizard glare, which is often delivered with both arms folded across her chest and the toe of her shoe tapping audibly on the linoleum kitchen floor.

There have been times that she'd looked a lot like an angry school teacher preparing to deal with an unruly student. This I've always found to be just too amusing to put me off. So I always walk right past her toward my wine cellar and simply enjoy a glass or two of vino while down there, below ground in my own private hideaway.

I make no direct eye contact with Eleanor when we do this little dance. Nor do I surrender the most minuscule second thought to the idea of self-deprivation.

The wine cellar itself is a peaceful sanctuary where I can hide from The Long Arm of Eleanor's Law. It's a sturdy shelter and its location muffles some of the sounds coming from above, both inside and outside of the house.

The acoustics are such that they lead voices and other clamor into a buffer zone created by a stretch of ceiling above the stairs, which lead down into the basement.

This part of the ceiling is not plastered over. So, noises are absorbed by the wood or flow into the cracks between boards and become somewhat muted. It isn't as good as actual soundproofing but it provides sufficient protection from the Bitch Brigade's bombs of bullshit.

I'm proud to say that I both designed and built the wine cellar entirely and did most of the physical labor myself. I remember, with some fondness, the days I'd spent digging out the initial foundation which I had decided to set in the earth beneath the existing concrete floor of the basement.

The idea being that wine was to be stored further below ground, where variations in temperature would occur more slowly. This subterranean environment would result in a more favorable atmosphere for proper aging. Creating these conditions was, however, a job that proved to be exceptionally difficult.

I had to shatter a section of the existing concrete basement floor with a jackhammer and then had to dig a hole into the earth beneath it.

I managed to create an opening twelve feet long by twelve feet wide and just a bit more than twelve feet deep. This hole would eventually become a ten by ten foot wine cellar.

Several dozen large fieldstones had to be removed from the ground in the process. Some of them were so large that they had to be broken into pieces in order to transport them out of the house.

Moving these rocks and manipulating the soil in which they had rested for centuries was very difficult. Mostly it was awkward. To keep one's balance on the uneven and freshly loosened soil underfoot while moving large heavy rocks would have been a trying experience even for a headstrong, farm-raised mule.

I do not consider myself a builder by nature. I am not a very physically strong person. But the end result of my labors is beautiful and will be enjoyed for years to come.

It's exceptionally impressive work, especially when one considers that the entire project was done based on pure speculation and with minimal assistance.

I'd gone in blind and weak but I did learn a few things in the process and gained a bit of strength along the way, after all.

The rocks exhumed during the process were put to use. Many were placed atop the fieldstones that make up a wall that divides my land from one of the bordering properties.

The stacked stones that make up the wall , born of the earth like fairy-tale dwarves, stand silent guard to this very day; unmoving as they keep an eyeless watch over the designated property line.

The stone wall itself provides a pandemonium of nooks and hidey holes for chipmunks, field mice, voles, moles, snakes, toads and other small denizens of the forest.

Salamanders, beetles and worms revel in the cool damp places beneath the wall's bottom layer of rocks that touch the soil and in the deep cracks between them where moisture has evaded evaporation.

Some of the stones are charming in the way that they resemble some sort of woodland furniture on display.

Some of the wide and flat stones are, at times, covered in decorative layers of browned pine needles; a table cloth set upon a long banquet table, in Mother Nature's dining hall.

Though at times exhausting, the physical part of the job proved to be a very enjoyable experience.

So, each day had left some satisfyingly visible mark of progression. And it had been frequent progression, like a child's increasing height marked off on a doorframe or the way a large breed puppy will put on ten pounds in less than a month.

It was work that also left me more physically fit. For the first time in years I felt that sort of exhilaration that sometimes accompanies manual labor. I had more stamina all around from putting my body to use on a regular basis.

With the help of my friend Donald, who is much more handy than myself, a ladder was built into the north wall. It is a fancy mahogany ladder. Its seven wood rungs lead down from the basement into the wine cellar, which after the paneling and racks had been put in, left me with a ten foot by ten foot room as planned.

There is a slightly eccentric air about this little room because I'd chosen to keep the floor earthen. I did, however, place a four foot by four foot piece of wood in the center of the room to provide a flat, solid surface for a small table and chair.

The wine-racks, which make up three of the walls, are also paneled with mahogany wood. The whole thing is quite solidly built and allows me to store much more than I need. But I am a collector - so, to have more than needed is really part of the enjoyment. In fact it's the overall point, really.

The racks themselves are something I'm exceptionally proud of. They are well made for their sole task.

They are designed and cut to hold the bottles at a thirty-seven degree angle. The bottles are also turned regularly. The thirty seven degree angle the racks are cut at and the turning of the bottles are measures of preventative care taken to avoid sedimentary build-up, which can ruin the wine.

The racks are also fairly decorative, almost pieces of art.

With the use of an electric woodcarving tool, I'd carved a bas-relief into several of the side-panels and baseboards. This is a simple, bold pattern that represents vines and leaves fairly well.

The racks are nearly perfect in my opinion. They are to the aging of my bottles of wine what a well-made arbor would be for the growth grapes that the wine itself is made of.

As I'd indicated, the room is occupied by a single, small wooden table and chair. Atop the table is a gas lantern, a box of long stem matches and a box of hurricane matches.

On a rack on the underside of the table I keep a couple of clean glasses with napkins tucked into them to keep dust out.

I also store a few books under there, so that when I'm in the mood I can sit and read and sip wine in the comfort of solitude and poetry.

A large volume of Robert Creeley's work is the only permanent literary resident, but there are always a few tomes readily available.

As previously stated, I have never been very good at building things, even balsa wood rubber-band powered planes have proven to be a formidable challenge in my bumbling hands. But, I think, even an experienced builder would have found the building of my wine cellar to be a challenge and I did a fine job for someone with so little experience at doing such things.

My friend Donald, the fellow who helped me install the ladder, agrees with me and there were, indeed, some challenges that nearly kept my private clubhouse from being completed.

The previous winter, storms had occurred quite frequently and several feet of snow had accumulated between late November and early to mid-March. When spring had finally arrived the accumulated crystalline blanket melted quickly, the frequent snowfall was replaced with a daily dose of pouring rain and as a result, the hole I was digging kept filling up with ground water.

At first this seemed like a blessing - because the soil and stones were loosened, but when the ground water really began to fill the holes ... well, the dirt became mud and was too loose to work with. So the job was not abandoned but it moved along slowly, following the water as it drained, seeping down into the earth.

Aside from the dilemma that Mother Nature had presented, there was another, more difficult obstacle to overcome - namely, Eleanor.

Ever so helpful and encouraging, Eleanor had stood like a statue beside the hole as I dug and had thrown negative remarks my way the entire time, and without just cause.

"You're not a builder, Howard" she had said repeatedly in that spine wrenching, parrot-like tone of hers. "You're a drinker, a stupid, lazy drinker."

Some days, I must confess, I was so discouraged and put out by her negativity that I would give up the project for that day and find something to do out of doors, just to be away from the bitch.

Sometimes, when retreat seemed the only option I would drive the country roads or walk around the forest aimlessly.

Though I had hated to give in to her, you must understand, a man can only take so much before he simply has to get away.

I'm not entirely sure why Eleanor had such a problem with my drinking but she certainly seemed dead set against my having a wine cellar. It is as if she were calling me an alcoholic.

I'll admit that I do enjoy a glass or two of wine a few nights a week, but by no stretch of the imagination am I, what most people would see as a drunk.

I suppose it's her father's doing. I do not know the entire story, and out of respect for her feelings have never pressed her for details.

But, as I understand it, Eleanor's father had been a heavy drinker. I know that her mother had been both physically and mentally abused during his alcohol induced fits of rage.

Though she has never spoken of anything happening to herself, I am sure that there must have been a time or two where Eleanor herself bore the brunt of these fits.

I am not, and never have been, a violent person by nature. It's been what seems like eons since I've even been in a fist fight or the tiniest scuffle.

Even an argument is a rare thing for me to take part in. Normally, I politely "agree to disagree" and let matters go at that. I know the taste of crow very well, so to speak.

The winter following the completion of the wine cellar was the first time I'd really gotten to fully enjoy it.

It was finished in fall and by December I'd stocked it with several bottles of wine and had set down the small table, chair and other creature comforts.

It was everything I'd anticipated and I grew to enjoy its sanctuary a bit more with each visit.

I also found pleasure in keeping a journal, written within the private confines of four underground walls.

It was late that winter when Eleanor and I had a very serious argument.

This argument had started while I was working on our screened-in back porch.

I had been feeling better from having gotten back into shape during the creation of my new sanctuary and had decided to keep busy so that my body would maintain flexibility and increased stamina.

Paint needed to be scraped from the interior of the porch so that it could be re-primed and painted at the start of spring and would be usable by summer when it was needed most.

There was satisfaction to be had in this work, but it was still a tiring and trying task to begin with and as I was scraping away, Eleanor was mulling about, tossing insults at me, making the word even harder to endure.

Her put-downs were delivered with the same sort of deliberation displayed in during my work on the wine cellar.

I did not ignore her this time. In fact, I dove into the rage. My brain shifted to an aggressive and hostile argumentative mode. After all, she would get more use out of the screen porch than I would. This was just damned selfish of her.

Before realizing I'd actually begun to speak I found myself hollering at her.

Nothing about the screen porch even left my mouth, at first. I stated my position on the wine cellar and on my enjoyment of the many bottles of wine that I'd spent MY hard earned money on and that she'd been nothing but a sore on my ass about it the entire time.

I went on to remind her the person she perpetually chose to call lazy was the only source of household income. To this, she had nothing to say in her defense and then the tears began to flow.

"Oh go on, cry. Cry, bitch, cry." I growled.

"Even your tears are selfish. Just for you, for nothing but the fact that you can't use the hair you have across YOUR ass to chafe a sore into MINE."

My words were well pronounced and sharp; each syllable a precision balanced vocal dagger - thrown with deadly accuracy.

My fingertips found my palms and closed into tight fists. I was talking with both my hands and my mouth.

I began gesticulating wildly. My arms involuntarily waved in at the air in front of me, as if my body were combating a swarm of invisible mosquitos that my brain chose to ignore.

"Howard," she said, stepping back, away from me, trying to look and sound afraid.

She'd even added a slight tremble to her voice that made the fear seem more convincing. But I wasn't buying it.

"Oh Eleanor" I thought to myself "you've learned much from watching television but very little from real life."

She began to speak again when I interrupted her explosively, screaming.

" SHUT UP AND LET ME TALK, YOU PLEASURE KILLING CUNT!"

I had shouted loud and had gotten right in her face, spittle flew from my mouth all over her. My hot heavy breath probably went up her nostrils.

Eleanor ran into the bedroom and locked the door. I could hear her sobs, they were muffled, as if she had her face buried in a pillow.

Suddenly I was embarrassed. I felt ashamed of myself for having lost my temper. I left the house for some air.

I Drove to a Mobile Gas station down the road from our house and bought a pack of American Spirit cigarettes and a twenty ounce cup of some heated diarrhea that they sell as coffee.

The smokes were the first I'd bought in years and I drove around chain smoking for hours and had burned through half of the pack before I returned home.

When I got home I pulled the car into the garage and shut off the engine. I sat there and smoked the other half of the pack.

I ended up falling asleep, sitting up in the car while listening to Art Bell's paranoid army of fans share their paranormal experiences. I dreamed that aliens invaded the planet and burned all of our fingers off.

When I woke up the next morning, cramped and aching, I found that I'd fallen asleep while smoking and that the cigarette had burned all the way down to the filter which still rested between my fingers. There were patches of a soiled saffron yellow along the two fingers that held it.

The ash was as long as a whole cigarette and fell to the floor as I turned my head to look at it.

After having thought the night through, I felt a bit guilty for pulling out the wildcard about the household money. Only because it had been established when we were married that she wanted to be an old fashioned "at home" type housewife.

I, being somewhat old fashioned embraced the idea because I desired the position of breadwinner. And the idea of having someone take care of all the menial tasks at home has its appeal. And then I'd chosen to throw it in her face to win an argument.

In retrospect it seemed below me. But I suppose it's typical; those who fill our environment often succeed in dragging us down without even trying.

When we try to look them in the eye we are forced to stoop to their level, often before we realize that we've stooped.

The argument went on in silence for several days. We tended to ourselves and gave each other space. We took our meals alone. I got some spare blankets and a pillow from the linen closet and slept on the couch without discussion.

After the fourth day of silence I felt some peace of mind and was able to think the situation over more thoroughly.

I came to the conclusion that Eleanor was probably jealous or felt left out so perhaps I could add some new feature to the basement or house to pacify her.

It surprised me that I hadn't considered this before I'd even started the basement.

In trying to think of what I could do to appease Eleanor, my mind immediately filled with images of food. For one thing, her hand in the kitchen has Midas's touch of gold.

She's such an excellent cook that for me to try and explain it would be below my means. Because, though I may be able to prepare a fine meal I'll never have the mastery of a kitchen that Eleanor has. She truly IS second to none with some foods, particularly her baked treats. She makes deserts and candies that would rival the confections of the famous Willy Wonka.

Eleanor was also more than proficient with an ability to can and preserve things.

She had a healthy garden. It produced the vegetables of every season and she harvested all of it. Those things that were not to be used immediately were preserved and stored. And when we ate them they did not taste like the can or the preservative, they were always well kept and delicious.

When it came to preparing game Eleanor maintained her status in the kitchen, that of a natural expert.

Behind our house the woods run deep and small game hunting is very good. Though I mostly go for pheasant and other game birds, I have bagged a couple of deer and more than my share of decent rabbits.

I would bring these home after having gutted and skinned them. Eleanor would not perform this task.

"It's just too ... too ... grisly!!!" she would always say, and she'd punctuate the statement with a forced shiver and draw in of the shoulders, as if the thought were so appalling it made her blood actually run cold.

She enjoyed sectioning the meats, curing them, marinating, smoking some of it and drying strips of it into jerky. Eleanor was good. She could even prepare duck in a way that it ended up being not as oily as duck usually turns out. She did this without a hitch and it seemed to take her no time at all.

I decided on building her a sort of larder, a place to store meats on hooks and canned and jarred items on shelves.

I began immediately, not getting much done at first, but doing enough to show her that I meant to finish it.

I managed to install one unfinished set of shelves and three large shiny meat hooks before showing it to her.

Because of our fight Eleanor had come nowhere near the basement and I was able to get this work done secretly.

That night I decided that we'd had enough of a break from each other. After all, our castle had become calm once again.

I approached Eleanor and asked politely if she would like to join me for dinner.

She didn't say anything, so I gave her a weak smile and told her I'd made too much anyway and that it came out well and that it would be a shame to waste a good meal.

She took the hint that I was sick of fighting, succumbed to the delicious aromas that my cooking had filled the house with and sat down to dine with me.

During our meal, which she agreed was delicious (and she wasn't just being polite, it came out damned good.), I told her that earlier in the day I realized that between my two projects I would be left with a lot of excess material. I didn't need it for anything in particular. So, I told her, I'd started to build a larder equipped with large meat hooks and a cupboard with a lot of shelving.

She was very surprised and seemed to please her.

"So that's what I've heard you doing down there." She said.

Eleanor began to speculate the larder's usefulness and talked of how she could hang meats and game for cutting and smoking. She smiled as she went on about the convenience of the shelving.

Finding places to keep things that do not get used immediately is always a problem for Eleanor.

In general her stores include hundreds of mason jars filled with preserved fruits and vegetables of all kinds. About half of these contain home-canned tomatoes as well as ground pumpkin and squash that she uses for pie filling in the fall.

Storage is always a problem for someone who revels in the hobby of food preservation in a passionate way. Something that Eleanor had always been known for.

"In fact ... " she said and paused while she pondered her constant storage dilemma. "Now that you've brought this up, Howard, I should tell you that I'll have to use your wine cellar to hold what will end up in the larder until you get it finished. That table and chair you have down there will have to go for the time being."

She looked at me and when she saw my surprise at these words she smirked and said "So don't dilly dally about it, Howard. You can be very lazy about getting things done, you know. So, the sooner you finish the sooner we'll both be happy."

She was still smiling as she got up from the table and went down the stairs into the basement to inspect my work. But, the charade was over. Eleanor was, at that point, wearing a cold-hearted, triumphant smile.

I sat, frozen in place, shocked. My hands were pressed down on the tabletop with enough force to make my fingers go white at the knuckles. My teeth clenched to the point that I could feel them pushing each other into my gums. I was speechless.

From the basement, Eleanor called up to me. What she said drew my shoulder blades together over vertebrae that now felt like an icicle.

My back muscles tightened up ... tightened up as she said "Oh Howard, this IS beautiful. But ... "

She raised her voice and annunciated each word with crisp clarity as she continued by saying "This ONE BIG HOOK will HAVE to go. The others are fine but THIS one... it's SO big."

There was a moment of silence and then Eleanor yelled "There's nothing for us to use it for anyway, Howard. I've thought about it and I don't think I want you bringing home even one more deer."

That night I began sleeping in our bedroom again.

As irony would have it, out of all of the hooks I'd installed the one that's ended up seeing the most use is "that one big hook that had to go."

In fact, Eleanor uses it each and every day.

Though, in retrospect I wish that I'd mounted it somewhere else. Because now each night as I make my way down the stairs to my prized collection of vintage wines I have to pass that hook and deal with her staring down at me.

She's looking rather pale and withered these days but with the help of some of her notes on keeping preserves - she keeps on keeping on, as they say. And, she still holds that trademark stare, that unblinking condescending reptilian expression that, in itself, says;

"Drinking AGAIN, Howard?!"

- 2006

after a passing storm

thunder claps
lightning bolts
made retreat to the sea

as the dog and I watched
at 3am
electric giants marched
along the river
        beyond
        a heron silhouetted
        against strange, gray
        backdrop smell of salt
        air mixed with   ozone
        of the storm   over
                              took
                              us
                              back home
                              enclosed
                              canine was manic
                              cat feared its shadow

                    in cedar chip habitats
                    rats were all hidden

                    one mouse of two
                    I found sound sleep

                    while the other
                    newly a mother
                    coddled her baby

                              - 2003

EEEYEP

figure paces
wears uneven
shades of impure
black shields to cover
neurotic in motion

as it weaves through cattle
all shower-clean and fragrant
out to graze on a new day, scattered

in fresh-start freeze behind books and papers
no heads, no faces - just hands and bodies

in crosshatched aura of grouch hysteria
a shark's potential swims a sea of scowls

here and there robots
shut down, in tilt
dragged under
by daily drone function
in slumber state
   nod off
   a bow in the court
   of nights true Lord
     Sleep
      The King
      that keeps

       vulnerable
       minds
       in need

        - 2004

As November Leaves

As November leaves
I go to the wind.

Ask it with my eyes
to carry me through

the air in slow circles.

Caught by the cold
updraft of breath

I'd weave between

> the many man-made,
> unnatural things
> that pollute and reshape
> the land's dead surface.

> Abominations that alter the path;

> tar on Mother Nature's lungs.

- 2003

The Hangin Tree

One summer, Grief played what was more like a handful of shows than an actual tour. All of the venues were on the east coast.

Between club-gigs, in Richmond, Virginia and Raleigh, North Carolina, we stayed with friends in Hayes Virginia and put on a house-show. It was more of a party with live music, on someone's private property, than a bona fide concert. It was a relaxed jam session in front of our friends, the other bands that played that night, the contacts who had set up the little tour for us and whoever they'd invited. There were also some stragglers who just showed up, having heard by word of mouth that bands were playing. It was an awesome time.

The place we played at in Hayes wasn't so much a house as it was an estate. It was an old plantation made up of several long white buildings.

As Terry pulled the van pulled off the main road and toward the house, I heard one of the guys from Seven Foot Spleen (I think it was Jon) tell Randy that the driveway of the place was two miles long from the front gate to the front door. Turned out he wasn't exaggerating. That dirt road seemed to go on forever.

It was night when we arrived and my recollection of the immediate surroundings is blurred from the hours of smoking pot that had occurred throughout that day. I remember it as being the kind of dark and spooky, winding country road you'd see in a scary movie.

The van's headlights lit the way before us, slowly revealing dirt road that meandered through darkness enhanced by overhanging tree-limbs, most of which were huge and must have been very old. I'm pretty sure that more than a few of these were ancient pecan trees.

A chorus of crickets and the strange sounds of unfamiliar night-bugs greeted us when the radio was shut off and the windows were rolled down. The air smelled thick with vegetation and moisture, like a shallow pond or a swamp.

The gig ended up being played in a building that was once used as slave quarters. Behind this structure there was a big, old tree where, we were told, slaves were actually "hanged by the neck til dead" (actually, I think I was told they were Hay-ang'd) if they got out of line, or whatever slaves did to earn death.

Jimmy from Jermflux was the first to mention the supposedly murderous monument to me. It came up during chatter that accompanied a joint we shared on a low, deck-like back-porch behind one of the buildings. He'd "heard the yarn" during his high school years.

The branch, supposedly used for noose-rope, loomed just beyond the porch. It reached out, overhead - spectral and ominous - in the electric-blue glow of bug-zapping-lights. The ground beneath it was almost entirely a lush, grassy area. The exception was a dark, lifeless patch of soil. This stood out sorely, directly below the spot where the rope would have been tied to the limb.

Something made me place myself on this lifeless patch of earth. When I did I felt a cold chill run from my ankles to my shoulders; a sensation that made me shiver. I immediately stepped out of the barren soil-circle. The words "blasted heath" entered my mind for a moment, spoken in an unfamiliar, droning voice.

I looked at Jimmy who, I think, gave me what I took as "an understanding nod" while he told me "Look up over your head, dude."

Campfire-story giggles came from a small, nearby crowd that had congregated by the back door that led to the deck-like porch. These people threw us sideways glances as they passed around a huge, dank, skunky smelling joint. Their laughter had a false quality. It sounded dry, like the forced laughter someone might retreat to when trying to suppress nervousness.

I looked up and saw that a ring-like depression had been worked into the limb. Bark appeared to have been rubbed away and then given time to grow back. It was like a large notch that started at the top of the branch, ran down the sides and around the bottom. It was like a concave strip, but wasn't as deep of a groove on the sides or the bottom as it was at the top.

I heard a nearby voice say "That ain't no natural dip." And I could see that it wasn't. Another joint was handed to me. I puffed away and stared up at the branch. The voice I'd heard went on to explain that the dip had been dug into the surface of the branch by a weighted rope over years of use.

After a few minutes of staring up at the branch against the night sky, a horrible, vivid picture entered my mind and stayed there; I could see a rope, like some sort of spectral reminder - horse-hair, pulled tight, creaking, something heavy swinging at the end of it; a morbid pendulum; the reflection a country's ugly past.

My mind's eye worked its way down the rope toward what I think was a body. At the knot I saw the top of a burlap bag, shaking and swinging back and forth. When I saw this the vision became too much for me to handle and I had to turn away. I was so creeped out that I actually shuddered!

A familiar female voice passed behind me in the darkness. Just out of view, she laughed and then said

"Oh, that's such bullshit. There was a tire-swing there for years when I was a little girl. That patch of dirt is all bare because it's where your feet hit the ground when you're sitting in the tire. It's where you'd push off to get swinging, Dumb-ass."

We smoked a third joint back there on the steps and Jimmy gave me a beautiful, black t-shirt with the cover of Jermflux's "Ruiner" 7-inch record on the front. This cover is an exceptionally erotic picture of a clueless-looking Nun lifting her robes to reveal enormous breasts in a candle-lit stone-walled chamber. Jimmy told me it was taken from some really old naughty story-book. I think he said it was written in French and had only a few illustrations in it, but I don't remember what the book was called ... or if he even told me.

I still wear that shirt. It's one of those quality shirts that not only fits perfectly, but the silk-screened image hasn't faded much over years of washing. And as an added bonus - the picture itself will timelessly piss people off.

The night's lineup included sets by Jermflux, Seven Foot Spleen (when they were still a four piece with their original vocalist, Jon) and us.

We played in this tiny little second floor room of The Slave Quarters - some spectators cramped in corners or seated around wherever they could squeeze in to listen, watch, smoke, drink and shoot the shit. A lot of people sat in the stairwell - using the steps themselves as little tables for beer, empty bottles and cans serving as ashtrays.

Cassette recordings of this show saw some local circulation and it became known as THE SOUTHERN BUD FEST. A friend, who we all referred to as "Uncle Grief" had taped the session. Did a good job, too.

That night someone had mentioned that we had smoked weed over fifty times since we'd woken up that morning.

Count had been kept by someone, starting at the 10am wake-and-bake joint session in a Waffle House parking lot - where four hung-over zombies had swayed tiredly, a joint was clumsily passed between them. Because of the awkward, over-cautious way they had handled it, an observer might have thought that the joint had weighed as much as a brick.

The tally had started there - at the dawn of the dead - and had been kept through the afternoon, evening and into the night.

We hadn't been let in on the fact that score was being maintained until the night was going full swing; everyone stoned and slowed down, grinning stupidly.

I can't verify that it was really fifty times, but it was a lot. I'm guessing realistically it was around thirty or thirty five times - which makes it understandable that someone would lose count in the first place. The person who had made that claim was a local named Zachary, I think.

Sadly (and very fucking strangely) I found out over the summer of 2001 that Zachary (or whoever ....) was mauled by a tiger in a freak accident at a traveling renaissance fair where he'd been making money for two years playing the lyre and selling honey-mead.

Aside from Zachary and maybe a dozen other unfamiliar faces, the only people in attendance for the entire night, really, were the bands and immediate friends of the bands.

Early on there were some girls there, but by the end of the night I don't think there was a single female anywhere near the place. I'd like to think there was but I don't think so; Curse of the Doom Metal Scene.

Aside from being drunk or stoned - almost everyone around us was on Valium. "The exceptionally yummy blue ones by Roche," someone had said. Many were also on Percocet.

Uncle Grief had gotten his prescriptions filled for his permanent back pains and at some point in the night he became The King Of Candy Land. He smiled as he walked around slowly, leaning on his walking stick like some dirty version of Gandalf and handed out magic buttons to anyone that wanted one.

At one point Uncle Grief asked Jeff if he could borrow a lighter. Jeff said "Yeah" and handed him one. It was a Marlboro lighter with a cowboy on it. Uncle Grief laughed about this and asked Jeff if he got that lighter as an attempt to "blend" with the locals. It was pretty funny.

While we played our set - we ended up in one of those mysterious scenarios wherein something about the room and the equipment set up remains un-grounded and certain things will give you a small electric shock. Jeff and I were both getting shocks off the microphones.

These shocks went through the lips and teeth and it was like your brains were being ripped out through your fillings.

Jeff got a good shock and dared me to put my teeth on the microphone.

I said "No way."

Randy laughed at both of us.

Terry started playing some Saint Vitus riff with his volume turned down very low.

Then,
Uncle Grief,
leaning on his walking-stick,
started shouting

"That's Right,
we're gonna Letra-cute all you Northanerz!"

- 2007

Stray Synesthesia

Falling rain strike sound;
taps of jelly beans
dropped into wax-paper bag.

Puddles grow.
Stop motion photography;
children, weeds, puppies, beards.

Ground glistens, under
sunlight - spattered
spectrums adrift here & there.

Autos slash through water,
hiss like black adders
sing secret snake songs.

City stink pushed down;
through cracks into pavement,
nose tainting odor makers

drowned in thin layer
on blacktop, stench of the moving
humans; leather, sweat and rubber.

Green life saps and roots
absorb what mud filters;
sky-milk for star dried fauna.

Soil separated spreads
rivulets run heavy
under the thunder.

(Stray Synesthesia, continued.)

Ears find magic
in umbrella concert hall, wet
tattoo by drummer unseen, overhead.

Chloroform artwork
rendered by no one's horsehair
brush outweighs classic graffiti.

Brilliant in its moment,
complexion contrasts,
clashes with gray overcast.

During embryo morning,
eye-reaching dew-glossed greens
shift in vision during dry up.

Pastel values dull
flatten, bled of shine
by heat.

Earth's epidermal frontiers,
ant battlefields forever
altered under weather.

Chaos carved candy
coating of the planet
upon which sweet life thrives.

Within nourished vermillion
kingdoms of poisonous
crimson berries flourish

Shrews catch crystalline
droplets as they fall
onto blood-stained, meat-fed tongues.

Grubs, slugs & worms
shimmer, tell of healthy
rich soil; abundant at present.

Beatles clamber over
under damp log;
on display seems sanded, glazed.

Marigolds breathe bitter air,
guards stationed
by rosebush base,

essential for survival
unseen, silent gas bombs burst,
defend baby buds from bugs.

- 2006

Acknowledgements

THUMBPRINT – was 1st published online at *Rockzillaworld's Americana Poetry Consortium,* 2002.

"Diseased" & **"Hurling coin"** were 1st published online at *Tim Peeler's Third Lung Review* # 32, 2002. They also appear in *Parallel Enigmas, Third Lung Press,* 2002.

"Ebenezer Oakman's House", **"Voices speak live and go"** and **"sometimes I wonder if I want them to"** are selections from *Parallel Enigmas* – a collection of poems written by Eric C. Harrison and Carter Monroe, published and printed by *Tim Peeler's Third Lung Press* 2003,

"No Rooster", **"So I Believe"** and **FC.**" Were 1st published in *The Underbeat Journa #2,* a deluxe printed literary zine, in July 2003.

"True Last Call" – 1st published online at *The-Hold,* 2003 and 1st printed in *Tyrannosaurus Rx* - Muertos & Pestle Press, 2004

"A Today of 23 Years" and **"Brown's House"** were 1st published online at *Jim Chandler's Thunder Sandwich #22,* 2003

"Warm Gift of Snow" and **"Paranoia Time"** were 1st published in *Tim Peeler's Third Lung review,* Print Edition, Issue # 34. 2004.

"Musical Midwives" & **"Wooden time Machine"** were 1st published online at *Jim Chandler's Thunder Sandwich,* #23, 2004.

"Shooting Star" was 1st published as part of *Glen Feulner's 63channels* printed, 12 month art & poetry calendar in 2004. **"Trod on Dead Being Gone"** was 1st published in the 2005 calendar.

 "Ligament from page 15" and **"In the midst"** are selections from *At The Bottom of The Big Top.* Published by *Marsh-Paw Press; 1st* in 2006 as a limited edition chapbook & again 2012 as a perfect-bound paperback book.

"Lost In Down-tuning" was 1st published online at *Tim Peeler's Third Lung Review* #36, 2005.

"Chapbook Chimney" was published as part of *Jim Chandler's "Goodnight Cait"* - a Cait Collins online memorial, in 2005.

"Near the Door", **"Ends In Silent Battle"**, **"Pink Mittens on The Train"** & **"Death Under the 107 Bridge"** – were 1st published in print in the 2005, Fall/Winter edition of *Glen Feulner's 63channels magazine*.

"The Hangin Tree" was 1st published in 2008 in *Load of Noise UK* – a printed fanzine based in Manchester, England.

"AOC Memory" – was 1st published online as "TKF Memory" in the last issue of *Glen Feulner's 63channels, 2010*.

"Dead Dragonflies" was 1st published in print as part of Pedro Trevino Ramirez's *Beat-Dog Broadside* in 2004

"Paradox" was 1st published online at at *Spitjaw Review* – a sadly short-lived on-line zine created by Pedro Trevino Ramirez. 2005

"Others", **"Walk WITH dog"**, **"Domestic Oasis"**, **"Trout Garden"**, **"to hear Pan"**, **"November 3rd, 2004"**, **"The Feel of The Bridge"**, **"ambivalent"**, **"Under The Arbor"**, **"caTHerINe"**, **"snowflakes Melt"**, **"in Massachusetts"**, **"Where Bees and Creatures Greet"**, **"caduceus coyote"**, **"after A Passing Storm"**, **"Eeeyep"** and **"As November Leaves"** were all 1st published online between 2003 and 2005 at *The-Hold.com* – a wonderful online zine created and maintained by the magnificent Cait Collins, RIP.

The short stories **"Howard & Eleanor"** & **"Chuckleberry Finn"** both appear in print here for the first time. Howard and Eleanor had been accepted for a publication that never ended up happening.

Some poems in this book were supposed to be in a chap-book called *"Dances With Justice."* It was to be a tribute to my old dog, Justice (RIP) and collected poems inspired by her or about places found when with her. The collection became too emotional to complete, too mentally taxing to finish. So, I've included some of the pieces in this book. These poems are noted in *"Dedications"* as *"for Justice."*

Dedications

About the cover art

The cover art is a drawing by **Nick Blinko;** a British, outsider artist diagnosed as suffering from schizoaffective disorder. Nick "draws things as he sees them" when not taking therapeutic medication, which impairs his ability to work.

Nick Blinko is represented in *The Collection de 'Art Brut, Lausanne* and *The Outsider Collection and Archive, London.* He also sees mention in *Colin Rhode's* book *"Outsider Art: Spontaneous Alternatives."*

Nick also has a book of his own art; *Visions of Pope Adrian The 37th* released by *David Tibet's Coptic Cat.*

The piece used for the cover of this book is *"Skeleton series # 6."* It is an ink drawing done on paper *"... around 2000, possibly earlier."* I bought this drawing about ten years ago from Nick Blinko through the **Henry Boxer gallery.** I recently obtained the permission from Mr. Boxer to reproduce it for the cover of this collection.

I've been a fan of Nick's art since about 1984 or 85 when I first saw it on an album cover; *Rudimentary Peni's "Death Church."* I paid 1.99 for the 12" record and still own the copy that I'd bought that day.

Aside from being one of my favorite artists, Nick Blinko has also written two books that I've enjoyed greatly – *The Primal Screamer (Spare Change Books)* and *The Haunted Head (Coptic Cat.)*

Nick is also profound lyricist and musician. He sings and plays guitar in The Rudimentary Peni, one of my all-time favorite bands.

So, for me, it is a true honor to have Nick Blinko's artwork on the cover of Picture of a Paranoid and my very heart-felt thanks go out to Nick and to Henry Boxer.

And ... should Nick ever read this – when renaming a file on my computer, during some stage of neurotic reorganization, I noticed that POAP (pope) could be an anagram for Picture of a Paranoid.

Nick Blinko is solely represented by The Henry Boxer Gallery, UK.
Check out the Henry Boxer Gallery online
www.outsiderart.co.uk/

Thanks.

When I started putting this collection together I didn't notice at first that it represents ten years of small press publications. When I did realize that, I had some fond memories of the friends who'd helped me along the way.

First off, thanks to anyone that has read any part of this book.

For all of their help with my words, I give enormous thanks to Carter Monroe and Tim Peeler more than anyone. They taught me to take being ridiculous more seriously.

Special thanks to Tim Peeler for having published some of my poems and for having helped me wrap my head around the Mark Twain references in Chuckleberry Finn.

Thanks to Jim Chandler for having published some of my work and for his helpful words that drove me to finish "At The Bottom of The Big top" and for a bit of help with an early draft of the short story "Howard and Eleanor." Also thanks to Jim for the brutally honest and helpful critique in online forums over the years.

Special thanks to Jennifer (Kardux) Dubin for reading AOC Memory with a pair of editor's eyes and for giving very helpful suggestions

Thanks, for supporting my words, by way of critique or publication also go out to Cait Collins, Mike Maguire, Glen Feulner, t.k. splake, Theodore Knapsack, Pedro Trevino Ramirez and Michael Johnson.

A very special thanks to all of my dogs - Justice, my old dog, RIP and Dargo and Chuck, the two pooches with me now. A lot of what you've read in this book came out of places and things I would not have discovered without them. They keep me going.

Thanks to Dean Koontz for both the massive amount of respect he gives to dogs in his stories as well as in real life and also for his acknowledgment of At the Bottom of The Big Top as something he enjoyed.

A very special thanks to Briana Piazza for helping me with this book and both of my art books. Without her support I may have never gotten them done.

Thanks to my friends Theresa McCauley, Jeff Hayward (& all the Grief guys...) Tony Yunta and Corey Bing for looking & listening when I've created something new.

Thanks to *anyone* who looked here expecting to see their name.

Thanks to anyone that has put up with my paranoia, delusions, anger and ... peculiarities. I'm not sorry for who or what I am, but I am sorry for a lot. I'm sorry for making up new lyrics to all of your favorite songs and singing them relentlessly and loudly. Constantly.

Eric C. Harrison is an American artist, writer & musician of international renown. He lives a fairly reclusive, nocturnal life in a drafty, but cozy, old house in a place that he calls Saltmarsh with two dogs, two turtles and a variety of small, generally unseen, furry critters. He is often approached by wild animals.

His artwork has appeared on vinyl albums of all sizes, picture discs, cd's and cassette tape covers. He has done movie story boards, book covers, chapbook covers and zine covers. His drawings and paintings have been printed in magazines, on posters, buttons, t-shirts etc. He has put out two books of art.

His written work includes Parallel Enigmas - a chapbook co-authored with Carter Monroe, At The Bottom Of The Big Top (a collection of poems that tell a horror story) and numerous poems, stories and short prose pieces published through a wide variety of literary zines - including The Underbeat Journal, Jim Chandler's Thunder Sandwich, Tim Peeler's Third Lung Review, The-Hold, Glen Feulner's 63channels Magazine, Spitjaw Review, Beatdog Broadside & Tyrannosaurus RX. Internationally, his writing has seen print through Mass Movement Zine out of Wales and Load of Noise in England. Eric was made a member of Rockzillaworld's Americana Poetry Consortium in 2002.

As a musician Eric has played on a number of CD's and vinyl albums and has performed live all over The United States and Europe. He is best known for having played bass and done vocals for GRIEF, a Boston based doom-metal band with a world-wide, cult-following.

On Grief's official website Harrison's reason for the band breaking up was partially due to his experiences with sporadic transformations wherein he would become part canine and was left unable to play bass due to ... having paws. He also claimed that this "canine lycanthropy" had caused his art to suffer.

"Eric finally became an actual dog and has not learned how to play bass or do artwork with his paws." – from an article posted on Blabbermouth linked from the band's Wikipedia page. March 1st, 2009

Apparently Harrison has broken that barrier as he is currently involved with two music projects; "Bad Life-Choices" a punk band in which he plays guitar, sings & sometimes plays drums and "B9K9" - an eclectic project, which Harrison founded and writes all of the music for. In B9K9 Eric usually plays guitar and sings, but also plays drums and a variety of odd instruments such as washboard, space-crickets, kazoo, rain-stick, tambourine, maracas, nose-flute, etc.

B9K9 L to R - Big D, Eric C. harrison, Chuck-Naked

www.ingramcontent.com/pod-product-compliance
Lightning Source LLC
Chambersburg PA
CBHW071133250626
47159CB00006B/2221